TALES FROM THE CRYPTKEEPER™

ISBN 0-590-25088-4

12 11 10 9 8 7 6 5 4 3 2 1 5 6 7 8 9/9 0/0

Printed in the U.S.A. 23

First Scholastic printing, May 1995

TALES FROM THE CRYPTKEEPER™

"Gone Fishin" and "A Little Body of Work"

Based on episodes of
Tales from the Cryptkeeper™

Adapted by Jane B. Mason

Illustrated by Erik Doescher

SCHOLASTIC INC.
NEW YORK TORONTO LONDON AUCKLAND SYDNEY

GONE
FISHIN

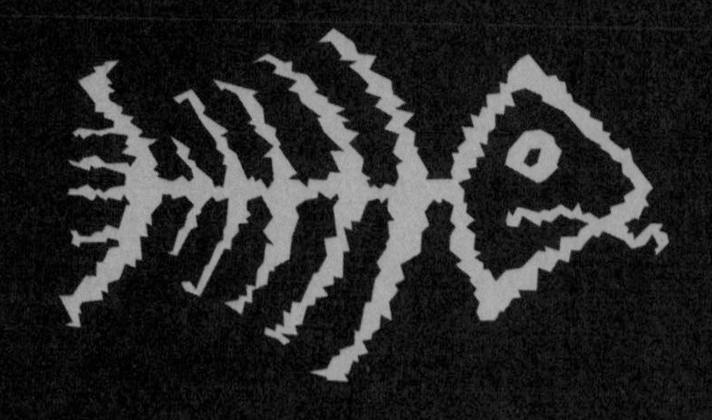

Hello Bones and Girls,

There's something fishy in the bass-ment. Hmmm, looks like they're not biting. But you will be — nail biting, that is! Here's a little nibble about our story. It's a lure-id tale that's guaranteed to hook your attention. I call it "GONE FISHIN"....

Randy and his uncle Ned were on a fishing trip. But Randy was more interested in reading about fish than seeing one dangling from a hook.

"I've got one!" Uncle Ned cried as his line went tight. An evil grin spread across his face as he started reeling the fish in.

Randy was too busy reading a book to pay attention. "Did you know they found a fish seven miles under the surface?" he asked his uncle.

Uncle Ned snatched the book away from his nephew. "That's the problem with you, Randy," he growled. "You've always got your nose stuffed in a book." He held the book over his head, then tossed it overboard. It fell into the lake with a splash and sank to the bottom.

“It’s time you learned what life was all about,” Uncle Ned continued as he went back to reeling the fish in. “It’s showing these bug-eyed slime buckets who’s boss!”

Just then the fish leaped out of the water and fell into Randy’s lap. “Aughhh!!” Randy cried in alarm.

“Quit being so squeamish!” Uncle Ned scolded. “Take the hook out!”

Randy looked down at the helpless fish. “It’s kind of small,” he said. “Can’t we just throw it back?”

“Why, so we can try to catch it again tomorrow?” Uncle Ned yanked the hook out and tossed the fish into a cooler at the back of the boat.

🐞 🐞 🐞

"How are we going to eat all these fish?" Randy asked his uncle as they pulled up to their dock later that afternoon.

"Eat! Are you kiddin?" Uncle Ned scoffed. He knocked over the cooler of fish and watched them fall to the ground.

"But Uncle Ned," Randy cried. "You can't just leave them there!"

"What's a pile of fish guts?" Uncle Ned shrugged and walked away.

🐞 🐞 🐞

That night in the cabin, Uncle Ned worked on his fishing lures while Randy dried the dinner dishes.

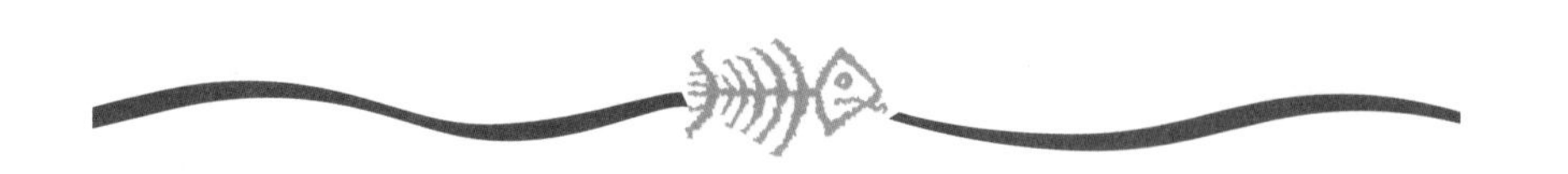

"Maybe way down deep the fish have their own world, just like we do," Randy said thoughtfully.

"That's just your problem, kid," Uncle Ned growled. "You're too busy imaginin' things to see the facts of life. If you take the bait, you pay the price!" He laughed a nasty laugh. "You'll learn. Now get to bed — and no reading!"

Randy crawled under the covers and turned on his flashlight. He just wanted to read for a little while....

Soon it was two o'clock in the morning. But Randy was too interested in his book to be tired. "One of the most peculiar species is the South American talking catfish," he read aloud, "which growls when removed from the water."

Randy's eyes widened as he read. This was really cool! But just as he shined his flashlight onto the next paragraph, a weird, squishy sound came from the doorway.

"Uncle Ned?" Randy called as he peeked out from behind the sheet.

Something stepped into the room, and Randy gasped. It was a giant catfish — wearing pajamas! It was staring right at him with cold fish-eyes, and its mouth kept opening and closing.

"Aughhh!!" Randy screamed. But when he looked again, the catfish was gone.

Randy blinked in confusion. "Weird," he mumbled. He pulled the covers over his head and went to sleep.

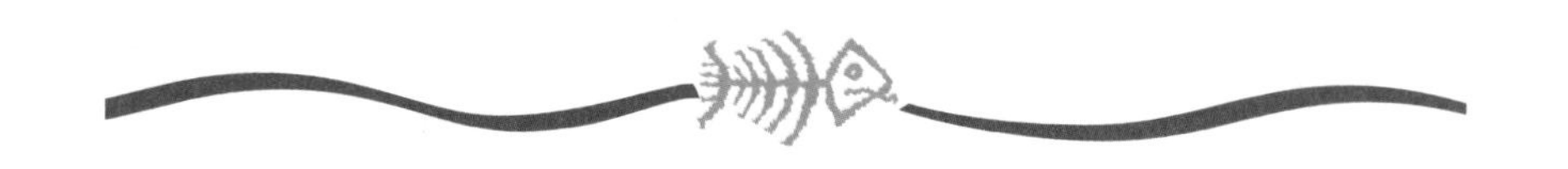

The next morning, Uncle Ned and Randy stopped at a bait shop to buy a few things.

"How're the fish biting?" asked the shop owner.

"Never better," Uncle Ned said as he picked up a new fishing reel. "I must've left fifty bass on the beach yesterday."

"On the beach?" The shopkeeper was shocked. "Even the best fishermen don't take more than they can eat."

"I had a weird dream last night about a catfish," Randy told the shopkeeper. "I think it was trying to tell me something."

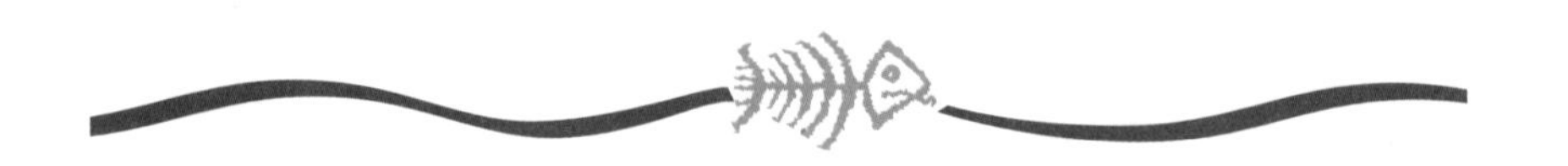

"Maybe it was," the shopkeeper replied. "The old ones say 'Nature speaks in many voices.' The wind rustling in the trees. The echo of ice shifting on the frozen lake. . . ."

"Now don't go fillin' his head with fool ideas," Uncle Ned interrupted as he started to cast his line. "He's got too many of those—ouch!" he cried. The hook was stuck in the seat of his pants.

He hopped around, howling in pain and trying to get free. "Don't just stand there," he shouted to the shop owner. "Get the hook out!"

WORMS

⁂

Later that day, Uncle Ned and Randy went out in the boat again. Randy still didn't want to fish, so he took the hook off his line when his uncle wasn't looking.

After a few minutes, Uncle Ned gave Randy a suspicious look. "Let me see that," he said.

Before Randy could resist, his uncle grabbed the rod and reeled it in. "No hook!" he cried as he held up the end of the line. His eyes narrowed as he looked at his nephew. "I'm gonna make sure you nail a fish if it's the last thing I do!" he declared.

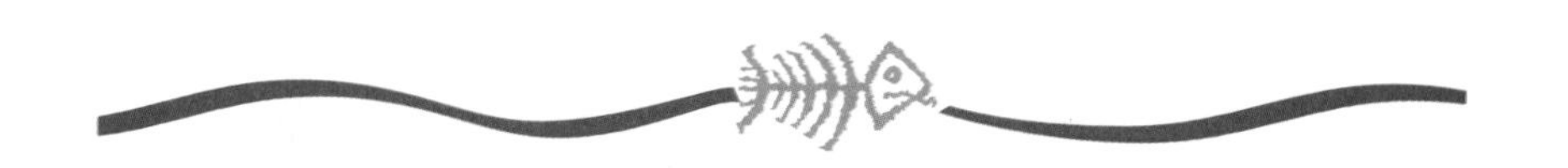

Uncle Ned tied a mean-looking lure onto the end of Randy's line. "Cast it," he ordered.

Reluctantly, Randy cast the line into the water.

A few moments later, the reel spun in Randy's hand.

"You got one, kid," Uncle Ned cried. "And he can't get away. The lure I gave you hooks 'em by the guts! But don't reel him in too fast or you'll snap the line."

Hearing his uncle's words, Randy began to reel in the line as fast as he could. He had to try and save the fish!

"Hey, what're you doin, kid?" Uncle Ned shouted. "I said you'll break the line!"

Randy reeled in the line even faster, and suddenly it snapped. The fish was free!

* * *

That night, Uncle Ned and Randy went out to dinner.

"I'm sorry, Uncle Ned," Randy said as he looked over the menu. "It's just that I really think the fish are trying to tell me something."

"I'll tell *you* something, boy," Uncle Ned said angrily. "We're going back out there first thing tomorrow."

Just then the waiter appeared to take their order. But when Randy looked up,

their waiter had turned into a giant catfish!

"Not again!" Randy cried in alarm. He jumped up and raced out of the restaurant into the night.

* * *

The next morning, Randy and Uncle Ned got ready to go fishing. Uncle Ned was still mad at his nephew for letting the fish get away, even though Randy had tried to apologize.

"I said you were gonna catch fish and I meant it!" Uncle Ned said firmly.

But Randy wasn't going fishing, no matter what his uncle said. "What you do is

wrong, Uncle Ned. And you have to stop or else — ”

“Or else what?” Uncle Ned challenged. “I’ve had it with you. Go wait for your parents at the bait shop.” He waved Randy away. “I’ve got some fishing to do.”

Just then Uncle Ned spotted a wallet sitting at the end of the dock. He snatched it up and stuffed it into his pocket. “Looks like it’s somebody’s unlucky day,” he said smugly.

He noticed the fishing line hanging out of his vest too late. Before he could react, the line jerked forward and Uncle Ned was yanked off his feet. “Yaaahhh!” he cried. He fell into the water with a huge splash.

At the bottom of the sea, a bass had just hooked a man and was reeling him in.

"But who knows, Uncle Gill?" said a smaller fish sitting next to him. "Maybe people have their own world up there on top of the land, just like ours."

"Stop daydreaming, Carpy," the bigger fish said gently.

"Are you going to catch any more today?" Carpy asked, looking up from his book.

"No. We have enough — a good mannerfish never catches more than he can *can*."

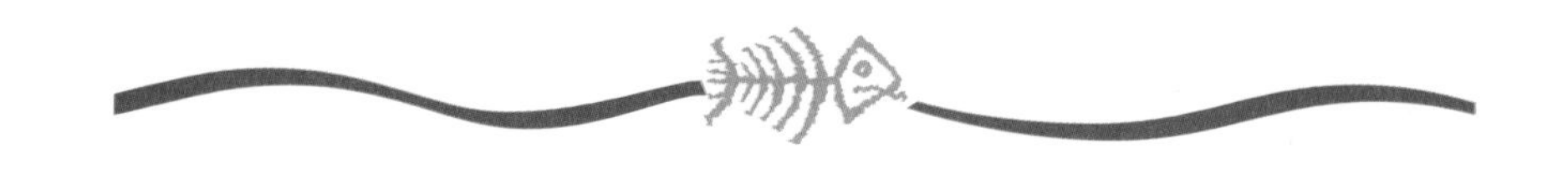

* * *

Weeks later, on a dark, quiet night, a small, round can washed ashore. The label showed a picture of a man — a man who looked exactly like Uncle Ned.

A hollow voice echoed from inside. "Hey, let me outta here!"

But it was too late. Uncle Ned was trapped forever. Because if you take the bait, you pay the price.

Kevin was in auto shop class, his head under the hood of a rusty old car he was rebuilding. “They might think I’m a fool for trying,” he told the car, “but I’ll get you up and running again.”

Suddenly, a loud blast trumpeted right next to Kevin’s ear. He jumped in surprise and banged his head on the underside of the hood. Looking up, he saw another student, Eddie, flashing him a nasty grin. But that was nothing new. Eddie always meant trouble.

“Gee, sorry, Kev,” Eddie said sarcastically. “Who’d have thought that the horn was the one thing on this car that worked?”

Eddie's friend Herman laughed.

Kevin ignored the dumb joke and gave his Mustang a pat. "I'm going to rebuild her."

"Are you kidding?" Eddie scoffed. "It's a pile of junk!"

Eddie leaned in to look at the engine, and suddenly the hood came slamming down. He stumbled backward and stepped onto a skateboard. "WWWaaahhh!" Eddie cried as he fell backward and landed in an oil pan with a splat.

The whole class cracked up.

Eddie glared at Kevin. "You'll never get this car runnin'," Eddie declared. He turned and left the classroom in a huff, Herman trailing behind him.

EXIT
OCTOBER

A few weeks later, Kevin's Mustang was almost ready to hit the streets. The car had a shiny paint job and the interior looked brand-new. Kevin just had to do a little more work on the engine.

"Ready for the big day?" Eddie asked, walking up to Kevin in auto class.

"What big day?" Kevin asked, not sure what Eddie was talking about.

"Our race, twerp," Eddie said.

Kevin shook his head. "No way, Eddie. I

didn't spend all this time fixing up my car just to race with you."

Eddie folded his arms across his chest and stepped toward Kevin. "You don't want to race 'cause you're chicken, and this pile of junk has no *guts*!" he practically shouted.

"Yeah, no guts," echoed Herman, walking up behind Eddie.

Kevin's face turned red with anger. He didn't want to race, but he was no chicken. And his car had plenty of guts. "You want to race?" he told Eddie, his eyes gleaming. "You're on!"

That night, Eddie and Herman snuck into the auto classroom and got to work on Eddie's 1971 Camaro. It was dark and spooky, but they had to get the car ready for the big race.

Herman read a printout from a machine that figured out what was wrong with the car. "It's in bad shape," he said, shaking his head. "We practically have to rebuild the whole thing. And we don't have the parts. What're we gonna do, Eddie?"

"Same thing we always do, Herman," Eddie said casually. "Steal 'em."

HOMEWORK
read pages

Later, Eddie and Herman went from car to car in town, stealing all kinds of parts.

"I don't know about this," Herman said nervously as Eddie quietly jacked up a car and slid underneath. "I mean, we're stealing major parts here. What if someone gets hurt?"

Eddie tinkered around underneath the car. A few minutes later he handed Herman a part. "Quit worryin'," he said. "Nobody's gonna get hurt."

He stood up and eased the car back

down to the ground with the jack. "C'mon," he told Herman as he picked up the rest of his tools. "We got lots more to get."

Later that week Eddie was working on his car while Herman read the newspaper. "'Rash of car accidents credited to clever thieves'!" he whispered nervously. "They know the cars crashed because we took the parts, Eddie!"

Herman was such a worrywart! Eddie thought. "Does it say 'Eddie and Herman took the parts'?" Eddie asked.

"Well, no," Herman admitted.

"We just need one more, Hermy," Eddie snickered. He turned to look at Kevin, who was putting the finishing touches on his Mustang. "And I know exactly where we're gonna get it...."

That night, Eddie and Herman snuck into the auto classroom. They opened the hood of Kevin's Mustang and Eddie peered at the engine. "Gimme a wrench," Eddie said when he'd found the part he planned to steal.

Suddenly, the car's horn blasted.

"Oof!" Eddie said as both boys whacked their heads on the underside of the hood.

A second later the headlights came on. "It's trying to blind me!" Herman whined.

"It's a car, Herman," Eddie said. "It can't hurt us. Now gimme that wrench."

It was the day of the big race, and both cars were at the starting line, ready to go. Herman stood between the cars, a checkered flag in his hands.

All of a sudden, Kevin's car coughed and died. Kevin turned the key, but the Mustang didn't start. Eddie grinned nas-

tily as he revved his Camaro's engine.

Kevin turned the key again, and the car sputtered to life. "Good girl," he said soothingly, patting the car's dashboard.

A second later Herman lowered the flag, and the two cars peeled out and headed down the road.

The cars were neck and neck as they roared down the straightaway. Eddie slammed his foot down on the gas pedal. "Come on, come on," he said anxiously.

"You can do it," Kevin said as he eased his foot down on the gas. The Mustang responded, inching ahead of Eddie's Camaro. Kevin was taking the lead!

Then, suddenly, a loud noise erupted from underneath the Mustang's hood. "Whoa!" Kevin cried as smoke began to pour out of the engine. He tried to steer the car straight, but it was spiraling out of control! He was going to crash!

At the last moment, Kevin threw open the door and rolled out, just as the Mustang crashed into the embankment.

Stunned, Kevin rolled over and looked up at his car — the car he had spent so much time rebuilding. It was totaled.

Eddie and Herman went out to Donut Burgers to celebrate their victory.

"I finally got even with that egghead Kevin," Eddie said, gloating. "Did you see how he acted when his wheels got totaled?"

"Yeah," Herman said. "It was like he lost his best friend!"

"He did!" Eddie howled.

Suddenly a car honked outside, and Eddie and Herman turned to see Kevin's Mustang parked in front of the restaurant — looking like new.

They stared at the car in shock. "How could he — " Herman began.

"Never mind how," Eddie said. "Guess

he didn't learn his lesson the first time."

He stormed outside and grabbed a crowbar from the backseat of his Camaro. But when he got closer to the Mustang, he realized that it was empty.

"Maybe it's a joke," Herman said.

"Well, we'll see who has the last laugh," Eddie replied as he threw open the door and leaped into the driver's seat. "Let's go for a ride!"

Herman jumped in the passenger seat. But before Eddie could put the car into gear, the doors slammed shut, locked, and the windows rolled up. In a flash, the seat belts snaked around them and tightly fastened both guys into their seats.

"Aaaaahhhhhh!" Eddie and Herman shrieked as the Mustang tore out of the parking lot and roared down the street. Eddie caught a glimpse of himself in the rearview mirror — but he had turned into a decaying zombie!

"The brakes, Eddie!" Herman shouted in a shaky voice. "Step on the brakes!" But when Eddie looked down, the bottom of the car had turned into a giant mouth with rows and rows of huge, sharp teeth!

"We're going to crash!" Herman screamed as the car veered into the junk-yard.

Then, suddenly, it stopped.

Del's
AUTO
DUMP

"Let's get out of here!" Eddie cried.

The two boys threw open the car doors and ran into the night.

"They're after us!" Eddie cried as the boys ran up to a police car that was sitting outside the junkyard.

"Don't let the cars get us!" Herman added.

"We took all those parts!" Eddie confessed. "The accidents were all our fault!"

Later that week, the newspaper had an interesting headline: *Car Thieves Walk to Jail.*

Kevin was glad that Eddie and Herman had finally gotten what they deserve, but he had other things to think about. He was already getting to work on a new car. And with the parts he'd salvaged from the wreck of his Mustang, he was sure he'd be able to put together a *very* special car....

Coming Soon...

Tales from the Cryptkeeper #2